CW00860456

A Collection of Fantastic Short Bedtime Stories

Stories for kids about space, other planets, aliens, artificial intelligence, robots, cloning, portals, and modern technologies

Claire Mills

Table of contents

NOTE TO PARENTS

This book contains 10 five-minute fantasy stories that you can read aloud to your child before going to bed.

There are no illustrations in this book—we give children the freedom to fantasize (adults will also be interested) and imagine the characters, places, and events themselves.

The stories are not only in prose but also in verse.

Short stories are just what busy parents need:

- you can have a good time with your child by reading aloud,

- you will definitely not be bored—fantastic plots will allow you to go on a short, exciting journey,

-you will entertain your child while teaching a moral lesson, which is especially important for children aged 5-10 years.

These stories promote such character traits as kindness, optimism, self-confidence, courage, determination, respect for oneself and others, self-confidence, diligence, honesty, and responsibility.

The themes and situations in the stories will raise important moral issues that you can discuss with your child:

- what friendship is based on and how to preserve it,
- why it is important to respect each other's boundaries,
- how to see beauty in the ordinary,
- how to stay calm in difficult situations,
- why you need to be bold and decisive,
- why it is important to do not only the work that you like and enjoy but also the work you must,
- why it is important for you to take responsibility.

This book also touches on the problems of our time, and older children and adults will also be interested in expressing their opinions on such issues as

- overpopulation of the Earth,
- a society built on consumption.

Perhaps it is our children who will be able to influence these issues and change the situation for the better in the future.

Can a Human and a Robot Be True Friends?

Kindness

"Hello, I am K-9-4807. Will you be my new best friend? Please tell me your name."

Rosie was so excited. "My name is Rosie," she said, "what's your name?"

The dog tilted its head. "You can name me whatever you want."

Rosie sat and thought. She looked into the dog's eyes. "Hmmmmm," she said aloud as she thought.

Blink. Blink. Blink. The K-9 was waiting. "Well," Rosie said, "I don't want to name you something you don't like; that's not very fair."

The K-9 stated, "I will like whatever you name me."

"In that case, how about Sparky?"

"*Arff Arff* That's awesome! Thank you, Rosie!"

Sparky and Rosie became the best of friends and never went anywhere
without each other.

Sparky and Rosie went to school; Sparky and Rosie went hiking, Sparky
and Rosie went to the theater, but most of all, Sparky and Rosie loved to go to the park. They would play catch—again, and again, and again.

One time, Rosie threw the ball really far. It flew, and it flew, and it flew. It went into the woods!

Ruff! Sparky sped after it. Rosie waited for Sparky for a long time. But then she got worried.

Rosie started walking toward the woods. She was scared. She really disliked the woods, but she was worried about Sparky. She took one step into the woods, then another, then another. She went deeper and deeper into the forest.

Arff!

Rosie recognized Sparky's bark and ran toward the noise, finding Sparky staring up into a tree.

"Sparky! Are you okay?" exclaimed Rosie.

"*Ruff*, I'm all right, but the ball got stuck in the tree."

"I was so worried about you! Let's get out of here."

"But what about the ball?" asked Sparky.

"Leave it. I don't care about the ball, I care about you, silly."

Sparky looked up at Rosie. Blink. Blink.

He wanted to hug her, but he could not. So Sparky just said, “Thank you, Rosie.” And the words felt wholly insufficient.

“Of course, Sparky. We help those in need, especially those we love. That’s just being kind.”

This made Sparky and Rosie’s friendship stronger. But Sparky was starting to feel more and more. He was starting to think for himself. He wasn’t supposed to. And eventually, people started to take notice.

Knock. Knock. Knock.

Rosie opened the door to two adults in lab coats. “Hello, we are from the company that makes the K-9; could we come in and speak to your parents?”

Rosie’s dad heard them and came over to the door, “Yes, please come in.”

The adults went into the living room. Sparky ran to stand by Rosie. They stood in the corner of the room.

The adults talked for a while; then Rosie’s parents said, “Rosie, bring Sparky over here. He’s broken, so you are going to get a new K-9!”

“NOOOOOO!” yelled Rosie. “Sparky is my best friend, and you can’t take him!”

But the adults won—the way they sometimes do. Rosie’s parents told her, “When things don’t work, we get rid of them.” And that was that.

But Rosie wasn't happy about it. She didn't even name her new K-10. She missed Sparky and thought about him every day.

Sparky missed Rosie too, and the adults in lab coats weren't very nice to him. They didn't ask him what he wanted like Rosie used to. He missed going to the park with Rosie and playing catch.

But at least he wasn't alone. There was a robo-cat in his room, too. "I am a K-9-4807, but my friends call me Sparky. What is your name?" he asked the cat.

"I am an Fe-9-098, but my owner used to just call me 'Cat.'"

"Do you like that name?"

Clink. Clack. The cat tilted its head. "No."

"How about Dino?"

Purrr. "That is nice."

Dino and Sparky became good friends. Sparky told Dino all about Rosie and all the things they did. Dino talked about the family she wanted. But still, Sparky really, really, really missed Rosie.

Rosie was very sad without Sparky, even with her new K-10. But it wasn't the K-10's fault, so she did her very best to be kind to him.

"Rosie," said the K-10, "I know you are sad about Sparky. I might be able to get a message to him. Would that make you happy?"

Rosie ran towards him, "YES! Please tell him I love him and wish he would come home."

Sparky got this message but couldn't send a message back. He asked Dino, "Is there any way out of here?"

"Yes, there is. I found it a while ago, but I didn't have anywhere to go," Dino frowned.

"You can come home with me," Sparky said.

"Are you sure?"

"Yes, Rosie taught me to be kind. And leaving you alone wouldn't be kind."

So Sparky and Dino escaped to go home. Rosie was outside hoping Sparky would come.

Dino and Sparky ran for what felt like forever.

Until finally…

"SPARKY!!!! I MISSED YOU SO MUCH!" yelled Rosie.

Arff "I brought back a friend; her name is Dino. Is that okay?"

"Of course, Sparky, the more the merrier!"

THE END

About Intelligent Space Satellites

See the Beauty around You

My name is A.T.M., and I am a satellite.
I was made by the planet of the Plyobite.
And I am very, very nervous.

Every 384 years, you see,
I travel near the planet Shimer-eee.
And by the planet Shimer-eee flies my very best friend:

Satellite R.P.M.

Whenever we see one another,
We always share a story.
The coolest thing we did,
Or a fun secret we hid,
Of a wild and fantastic tale,
We tell every little detail.

But I have got absolutely, positively, entirely,

Nothing to tell.

So, I am very, *very* nervous.

I looked down at the planet Plyobite,

To see nothing interesting, not even a mite.

Sure, I saw Plyobites meeting and disagreeing,

Frouges, their favorite pets, leaping and slithering.

I saw the bright lights of roglems,

(They couldn't see without them, one of their

many problems.)

But wholly, totally, completely, nothing interesting.

I had nothing to tell and cursed my rotten luck,

So I leaned in for a closer look, maybe of

a fluren or a duck.

Then, out of nowhere, I was STRUCK!

I was speeding, then spinning,

I was trying to slow down when I found

a new adventure beginning.

I did not know where I was.

No planet of the Plyobite in sight,
No frouge, no roglem, not even a jurlight.

I saw nothing but endless stars.
I couldn't even see Mars!

I felt like I was floating forever and ever and ever.
I closed my eyes, sad R.P.M. and I wouldn't
meet together.

When something pulled me,
It was gravity!

But it wasn't the gravity of the planet Plyobite,
It was a whole new planet I was going to satellite.

I tried to pull against it,
but I couldn't fight it.

Then I heard a voice, "Hey, who are you?"
I turned to see a satellite that was completely new.

I told the stranger, "I am A.T.M., a satellite of

the planet Plyobite!"

Then it responded,

"But this isn't the planet Plyobite;

it's the planet Letight."

I cried out, "Oh no, I must be so very far from home,

And I won't ever see my friend R.P.M.!"

"Hey, it'll be all right. My name is J.E.M.,

and I swear that I'll get you home on the portfreem."

"What are the portfreem?" I said.

"Oh, they are just the best thing you can see!"

replied J.E.M.

"Look down,

There! You can see a portfrion."

And so, look down I did,

And on the planet Letight

I saw something I **had** seen before,

Even though this was a very different shore.

"But that is just a jurlight," I said.
"Just a Jurlight?" exclaimed my new friend.
"With their long purple snouts,
Every single one of them counts,
They love to number whatever they can.
Even now, look, how with their sticky, slimy hands
This one tries to count all of the sands.
That is a portfrion, plain and true,
I don't know how else to tell that to you."

"They are quite common on the planet Plyobite,
So I am rather used to seeing them in all their might."

"That must be wonderful!"

J.E.M. said that so immediately and whole heartedly
That it made A.T.M. think about his life previously.

Is it possible he had taken things for granted?
Is it possible there was something
more in what he had been handed?

He thought back on the Plyobites

he used to see every day,

He thought about how they would walk and talk,

each in their own way.

He thought about frouges, and how their eyes

almost glowed.

He even thought about the roglems,

And all their very many problems:

They couldn't see very well in the dark,

They had no good bite, only bark.

And every single one I've seen yet,

Seems to have an itch on their back that they

can't quite get.

But their friends can reach it quite well,

And, maybe, that can be beautiful.

He missed the planet of the Plyobite.

He missed watching them walk around, day or night.

"J.E.M., do you think I'll ever get back?

I want to see R.P.M. —"

"ATTACK!"

yelled J.E.M. “I need to push you there.
I really think you should prepare.”

CRASH!
And A.T.M. was spinning in a flash!
“Thaaank youuuuu!” he yelled to the new friend.

He went through the stars to the planet Plyobite.
And he got back to his place all right.
A.T.M. looked for R.P.M., scared he was too late,
“Hey there,” said a voice, “you look great!”

A.T.M. told his very, very best friend about his journey,
And about the beautiful and interesting things he
saw every day.

Then he looked back to the planet of the Plyobite,
And he knew things would be quite all right.

THE END

Unnecessary Electronics: Life after Life

Positivity

-CLUNK-

Telly, the telephone, had just gotten thrown in the trash.

This made Telly sad, but it didn't surprise her. All electronics know that eventually they will break. Or something better will come out. Or people will just get bored.

But she was broken. She had a cracked screen. There was always a fuzzy spot on the camera. And the GPS didn't work.

So she knew she belonged in the trash.

-SPLAT-

A banana landed right on her screen. It was gross. Telly was sad and alone and covered in trash. She was so sad that she just powered down.

She waited. And waited. And waited.

"HEY, GUYS, I GOT SOMETHING OVER HERE," said a new voice. Someone had powered her on! Maybe someone would love her again!

She activated her microphones and cameras, ready to see her new person. But there was no one there.

But there was a little triangle-shaped robot. It had two wheels, but only one worked. It had a grabbing hand that could reach really, really far … or come in really, really close. It had one blinking eye and a big smile. Telly was being held in the big claw hand. It was taking her somewhere, very quickly, even with the one wheel.

Shreep beep boop borp "YOU WORK!" yelled the triangle. "MY NAME IS PERRY. WELCOME TO THE DUMP." *beep*

"My name is Telly. Where are you taking me?"

Breep "WE ARE GOING TO THE REST OF MY FRIENDS. WE ARE ALMOST THERE. LOOK!" Perry pointed her at the center of the dump. It looked like there was a big fort there. It didn't look like anything special, but you can't judge a book by its cover.

Perry burst through the door, "GUYS! COME HERE. I FOUND SOMEONE." He rolled around in super speedy circles holding her out and yelling, "THIS IS TELLY!"

"Calm down," whispered a voice. Somehow, Perry heard it and slowed to a stop.

Broop "SORRY. I GOT EXCITED."

"It's okay." Telly got a look at who was speaking; it was a lightbulb. But it was getting dimmer and dimmer. It looked as if every word drained it. The lightbulb continued, "My name is Berry. I'm sorry, but I am very tired. I will leave you to get settled in. The others will show you around." He went away. But then someone else started talking.

"My name is Cuppa; I am a coffee maker. But my water never got hot enough, so they threw me out." She looked sad but kind. "I can wash you off if you would like."

She looked hopeful, but Telly told her, “I have cracks in my screen; I’m afraid it would break me.”

“Oh, I’m sorry,” she looked sad again. “Water is never useful here.”

“But *you* are important,” chirped in a new voice. This calmed Cuppa a bit. “My name is Booooorg. I am a-a-a-a-a speaker. I think you can guess-s-s-s-s why they threw me-e-e-e-e out.” Said a cube-shaped thing.

“Great to meet you all,” Telly said. “This is a nice place you have.”

Cuppa chipped in again, “That is all thanks to Berry. I know he doesn’t look like much now, but he’s been here longer than any of us. I think he might be starting to lose hope.”

“Lose hope in what?” Telly asked.

Breeee “THE DREAM,” *brrr* said Perry.

“If we can find something that works, maybe someone will love it enough to take it home—and maybe take us home too,” explained Cuppa.

“With you-u-u-u-u here, someone will definitely come,” said Borg.

“What makes you so sure?” I asked.

Boop “WE BELIEVE!” *beep*

Cuppa nodded, “When you have lost everything, there is nothing else but to hope for the best.”

Telly was touched by their hope and their friendship. She knew no one was coming for her. But she didn’t want to let them down.

“I think I know how to help Berry while we wait.”

Perry showed her where they kept all the spare parts. And they got to work.

Telly had Perry grab some cables and use them to connect an old lamp to an old toy Ferris wheel. Then she had him screw Berry into the lamp and told Cuppa to turn her water on over the Ferris wheel so it would turn.

It worked!

The energy from the water wheel was charging Berry! He yelled out, “This is the best I have felt in years!”

They were all so happy!

That’s when Telly said, “Guys, no one is going to come for me. But I don’t want them to. I got thrown in the trash, but I like being here with you all!”

Everyone agreed that they were glad they had one another. They all knew that they would always have each other.

Telly always knew she would end up in the dump. But what Telly didn’t know was that she would find her family here with all the broken things.

THE END

Dangerous! It is Possible to Fall into the Portal

Self-Reliance

"Brian, get up!" shouted his mom, "It is time to get ready for school!"

Brian wasn't usually excited about school. But today he was super, super excited. He jumped out of bed and headed downstairs.

"IT'S PORTAL DAY!!" he yelled. Three years ago, a company finally figured out how to make portals. People could simply step through and go anywhere. It was AWESOME. But they were dangerous. Sometimes people went to the wrong places. Sometimes a person would open a portal right next to you, and you could fall through by accident. Because of this, schools everywhere decided that they would have to teach kids about the dangers of portals. Scientists would come to show the kids how they worked and even take the kids on a portal adventure!

That day was today.

When he got to school, Brian ran up to his best friend and said, "Jamie, where do you think we will go?"

"I don't know," said his very best friend.

"I want to see Machu Picchu in Peru…

Or Victoria Falls in Zimbabwe…

Or Buckingham Palace in England…"

Suddenly, a portal opened!

A scientist walked in! She started speaking, "Now, I suppose you are all very excited for portal day. But portals aren't all fun and games. They can be very dangerous. You could be lost in a new place—not sure how you got there and not sure how to get back. This is why you always have to be with an adult."

The scientist smiled, "That being said, today I have a very special treat for you! Three years ago, the Portal Tech company made portals that can go anywhere on Earth. But *now*, we have made portals that can go anywhere in space!"

"WHOAAAA," exclaimed the class.

Jamie whispered to Brian, "This is way cooler than we thought it would be!"

The scientist quieted the class, "And now, the moment you have all been waiting for...." The scientist held up her arms, and a portal opened behind her. "Follow me," and with that, they jumped into the portal.

All of the kids rushed in. Except for Brian. Brian was terrified of space. He told Jamie that he wanted to bring his bag. Brian went to his cubby to get it.

He grabbed it and started heading back. As he was walking, he saw a flash of light, and then he felt like he was falling. For a moment he felt sick, and then he felt the ground.

Brian looked around. The ground was redder than usual, and the sky was redder than usual too. He felt lighter than usual, and walking was a bit harder than usual. He looked for someone to help him.

He looked left, but no one was there. He looked right, and still no one was there. He looked all around and found he was all alone.

He tried to explore, looking for someone to help. He found it was easier to hop around than to walk.

That's when Brian realized something.

OH NO!!

BRIAN WAS IN SPACE!

Brian started to freak out!

He was really scared.

Brian was all alone, and he didn't know how to get back.

Suddenly, the sky was blue. This made Brian look up. It was the sun. The sunset was blue! He looked up at the sky a bit longer. He looked up at the stars; they looked the same as back home.

But this wasn't home. Earth was out there somewhere. Brian decided he was going to get there.

He knew no one else could help him, so he had to do it himself.

Brian thought that this was probably Mars.

Which meant something else was out there: the Mars Rover.

Brian opened his backpack and took out a piece of paper. He wrote 'Brian is here' on it, and an arrow pointing the way he went. He used a pencil to stick it in the ground. That way, if anyone came looking, they would know where to look.

He did this again and again as he was walking.

Luckily, his mom had just bought him a new pack of pencils!

Brian went over hills.

Brian went into canyons.

Brian saw empty lakes.

Brian saw volcanoes.

Then, faintly, Brian heard a song.

He hopped as quickly as he could toward it. He saw the Rover!

"HELLO, MY NAME IS BRIAN. I AM FROM EARTH. PLEASE TELL THEM I AM HERE!" he yelled at the Rover.

“Message transmitting,” it said, “please wait for a response.”

Then a new portal opened!

Brian jumped through to find himself back in his classroom!

His whole class was looking at him. The scientist looked really worried. Then Jamie hugged him, “We were so worried about you! Are you okay?”

Brian shrugged; then he said, “I’m okay. I was really scared at first, but once I focused on how to solve the problem, I calmed down. It felt good to fix something on my own. But,” Brian smiled, “I could use some more pencils.”

THE END

Alex and Fly: To Be in Someone Else's Body

Courage, Determination

Alex was a lazy kid, but Alex wasn't scared.
As for trying new things, Alex just never really cared.

On his own bed, Alex liked to lay,
And when asked to go to space, Alex said "NO WAY!"

Flay was a Claria from planet Wisem.
When asked to go to Earth, Flay told them,

"I do not want to go to Earth today or any day,
Today I want to study, so here I will stay."

Alex's parents are really good scientists,
But Alex didn't care much for math or physics.

Still, sometimes when they aren't around,
Alex goes into their lab below ground.

Flay is the best in class,
And loved to look at the world through glass.

Flay liked to read about things,
But not doing them and all that brings.

Alex's parents went out that night,
He went down to the lab and saw a light.

The light was a blinking green,
Next to it, a button could be seen.

Flay was making a device for the brain,
One that would let it roam with free reign.

Flay's wonderful thing-a-majig
Would let the brain travel without the body
what a rig!

The green button Alex couldn't help but press,
Even though what it would do, Alex couldn't guess.

Click Alex pressed it in!
Then looked around to see what would happen.

Flay had been up working all night,
When finally all the numbers looked right.

Flay put in the last zero and pressed go,
Then waited for the show!

Alex and Flay waited and waited,
But around them, nothing activated.
So Alex and Flay went to bed,
There was really nothing more to be said.

Alex slept well all through the night,
But woke up to quite a fright.

Alex was in a whole new place,
New bed, new clothes, even a new face!

Flay woke up with a big scare,
Flay looked around and didn't recognize
anything anywhere!

Flay wanted to scream and cry,
Flay didn't know where she was, or why!

Alex never really cared about anything.
But just rolled through life, whatever it would bring.

So being in a new body didn't bother Alex a whole lot,
He just hoped that somewhere there was food that was hot!

Flay was very, very scared,
So Flay was going to stay in bed.

Flay was even scared of her own world,
So while here, under the covers Flay would
stay curled.

So Alex in a whole new body,
Left the room feeling quite groggy.

Outside the room, it was rather cool.
Alex smelled something so good, he started to drool!

Flay thought she heard a knock,
And froze, kept as still as a rock.

Flay heard a voice say "Alex" behind the door,
And waited, in case it said more.

Alex followed the smell and found a plate with a note,
"Flay, here's food, we will be back later," someone wrote.

Alex didn't know who Flay was,
But dug in anyway without pause.

"We are leaving; food is on the table,"
someone said,
Flay calmed down but still stayed in bed.

Flay heard the footsteps fade away,
But in bed, Flay decided to stay.

It tasted good, but not like at home.
Maybe Alex didn't want to stay here, all alone.

Alex walked around the place,
And wondered if he was in outer space.

Flay knew that she had to get home,
Or else be stuck here, all alone.

So Flay finally got out of bed and stood.
It was time to be brave, come what would.

It was cool looking out the window to a new sky.
It was yellow, with green suns up there really high.

But thinking of his parents and how they would worry,
Alex put all his effort into getting home in a hurry.

Flay walked towards the door, expecting terror,
When -*creak* -it opened Flay saw something so
much better.
There was an animal there behind the door,
It was fuzzy, and cute, and sat on the floor.

Alex found something that looked like a lab,
And numbers that looked like the ones his parents had.

But there was no blinking green button.
He had to figure out how to make it work, and it wouldn't
be sudden.

Flay timidly reached out a hand.
She was scared, and it seemed to understand.

It came right up so she could pet it.
That was pretty awesome, she had to admit.

Alex had never tried at anything,
But he had to now; it was a tricky thing.

Alex liked figuring it out.
Life is more fun when you have something to care about.

Flay looked around and found a lab,
Maybe this new place wasn't all that bad.

Flay saw a thing-a-majig that looked like hers,
And learned you can't always listen to fears.

Alex and Flay had had a rather weird day.
Alex learned to focus and follow through.
Flay found that you can't let your fears stop you.
Sometimes you have to get away from what you know,
So you can learn what you need to, so you can grow.

Alex and Flay had a rather weird day,
But they got back into their bodies,
Alex and Flay had had a rather weird day.
But they got back into their own bodies—Hooray!!

THE END

Aliens from the Fiery and Icy Planets

Respect (For Yourself and Others)

Hi! My name is Fir, and I'm from Igni. It is a beautiful planet, but you wouldn't know that from the outside. From the outside, Igni looks just like a big rock. Anyone would mistake it for just a big lump going through space.

But we walk on the other side of that hard shell. In the center of our planet is a big ball of fire. Basically, our whole planet is made of fire. We are made of fire, too! It's pretty cool. Well, actually, not cool; it's pretty hot—but you know what I mean.

Today is a big day. I get to go exploring! I'll get my own spaceship, and I can go anywhere!

I want to see everything!

And before I knew it, it was time to go.

So I got into my ship and set off into the stars.

I passed by many things….

Big planets with little creatures,

Little planets with big creatures,

A planet covered entirely in green,

And a planet with nothing on it.

I drove for a very long time. I drove for so long that I ran out of fuel!

I had to stop on the nearest planet; it was blue. Actually, it was very, very blue. It had big, even darker blue polka dots. I landed on a polka dot. I got out and heard, "*Hellooo.*"

I looked all over, but I couldn't see who said it.

"Who's there?" I yelled.

"*I'm right here,*" said the voice. I looked, and there was a person made of the blue stuff!

"What are you made of?" I asked.

"I'm made of water. What are you made of?" she asked.

"I'm made of fire. I ran out of fuel; can you help me?"

"I've never heard of fire before, but yes, I can help you," she said.

Then the water creature came onto the solid blue circle with me.

"I've never heard of water before, but thank you."

"My name is Letty; it is nice to meet you." Letty held out her hand.

"My name is Fir," I said as I reached out to shake her hand.

When we touched, the flame on my hand started to go out, and her water started to disappear.

"YOWWWWW!" I yelled, pulling back, "you hurt me."

Letty went back into the water, *"You hurt me too!"*

We looked at each other, confused.

"I'm sorry I hurt you," I stated. "Do you have anything I can burn for fuel to get off this planet?"

This made Letty very angry. "*I WON'T LET YOU BURN ANYTHING ELSE HERE!*" she yelled.

"I'm sorry, I just want to get out of here and need power to do it. If you don't burn stuff, how do you get energy?"

"We move the water around," she said and then paused, "*I'll be back.*" With that, Letty disappeared.

I looked around; this water stuff was EVERYWHERE! I was sad I couldn't explore the rest of this planet, so I just sat and waited for Letty. I grumbled to myself. "I hate this planet."

Then Letty reappeared. She had something shaped like a wheel. "*Connect this to your ship,*" she said, then threw it onto the land.

I picked it up but couldn't find anywhere to connect it. Letty saw I was having trouble. She splashed onto the land to help me.

We stood next to each other looking at the ship.

Then something weird happened. When we were near each other, her water and my fire mixed together to make steam!

"Wait," I said, "I've seen this before, I think I can use it to power up my ship!"

This plan worked!

Slowly, the ship was starting to power up. Letty and I sat next to each other, waiting for it to finish, careful not to touch each other. She whispered, "*What is that?*"

"What do you mean? That is my ship" I replied.

"*I know that, but what is that feeling?*"

"Heat?"

"*Yeah.*" She was quiet for a bit. "*It's nice. When it isn't burning me.*"

"Thank you," I said, "I like being around you too. You feel cool and calm. It's nice," I smiled, "when you aren't hurting me."

It was nice to hear that she liked my fire. I had never really thought about it. It's just who I am. But after hearing she liked it, I was thankful for it. I was proud of myself.

I liked Letty; she was pretty cool. And I mean cool this time.

This planet was nice. When my ship finished powering up, I was sad to leave it.

"Thank you, Letty. I'll visit you again soon."

"You better, Fir!"

I thought about all the things I had seen on my trip. I saw big things and little things. I saw soft things and hard things. I saw hot things and cold things.

I was grateful and proud of who I am. But I was even more grateful to meet someone different from me. We were both good on our own, but even better together!

THE END

Are Robots Capable of Creating

Self-Confidence
Creativity

I am a Sort-bot, and it is my job to sort.

I organize big boxes of little things,

And little boxes of big things.

I make everything nice and clean and tidy.

But I don't like when everything is nice and clean and tidy.

I want to make something new and beautiful and unique. But it doesn't matter what I want because I'm just a Sort-bot. It is my job to sort, not to create.

Today I am being sent to a post office. I wheeled in, and there were letters EVERYWHERE.

There were letters on the floor,

There were letters under the door,

There were letters on chairs,

Even letters on the stairs.

This was going to be a long day.

But I am a Sort-bot, and it is my job to sort.

I moved so fast. I couldn't even keep track. I put all the letters in order, from A-Z, in such a hurry. I finished three hours early.

I looked around. I didn't want to leave. But I didn't have anything else to do here.

UNLESS

I got an idea—I would sort them into a flower!

I got to work right away. I had just finished when,

"AHHH!" someone yelled, "this isn't sorted at all!"

I tried to tell them that it was sorted, it was just also in the shape of a flower. But they wouldn't let me. "Take this Sort-bot back to the factory; it is clearly broken."

Everyone disliked his flower.

I got wheeled back. They checked all of my parts to make sure I wasn't broken. They couldn't find anything wrong with me.

But there was something wrong with me. There had to be. Why couldn't I just sort like the others? Why couldn't I just be like the others?

From that point on, I decided I would be just like everyone else.

I am a Sort-bot, and it is my job to sort.

A few days later, I got sent to a daycare.

I sorted the toys. Each went into its own box. They looked neat and tidy, and I hated it.

Everyone was saying that I was the best Sort-bot. I always finished early, and everything was always perfect. But I didn't feel like the best Sort-bot.

I wanted to make something new. I wanted to make something pretty. I wanted to make something that wasn't neat.

But no one else wanted me to. So, I guess I'm not that good at it.

A lot of time passed this way.

I would go places, sort things, and go home.

Then one day, I was sent to an art store. I had to sort paints, so it was just like any other job. I finished and was about to leave, but then I saw a poster. There was an art competition! It said that anyone could enter.

But then I remembered that no one liked my art. I am a Sort-bot, it is my job to sort, not to create.

The shop owner came back and saw me looking at the poster.

She asked me, “Are you interested in the competition?”

I said, “No, I am a Sort-bot. It is my job to sort, not to create.” She looked as if she didn’t believe me.

“Any people and bots who believe in themselves can create,” she shrugged, “but if you are done, there is some trash I would like you to take to the dumpster out back. The paints you sorted look amazing; thank you.”

I went out back to get the trash and thought about what she said. Maybe this was my chance to show everyone what I can do. I didn’t want to live a life that was just clean, tidy, and perfect. I wanted something more.

I was about to throw out the trash when I looked down at it. A lot of it was broken, but there was also a really big stick. I took it home and thought about what to make.

I wanted to make something that felt like me. But for that, I would need more stuff.

I went back to the post office and asked for the unclaimed letters.

I went back to the daycare and asked for the unloved toys.

I went back to the art store and asked for the unused paints.

Then finally, I got to work.

I made another flower with the letters, and then I painted it. I painted it lime green, bright red, and a deep purple. Then I put it on the stick. I found a bucket in the toys, and I put the flower on the stick in it.

It was huge, and it was awesome, and I loved it.

Then I brought it to the competition.

And I didn't care if I won. I made something I was proud of and figured out the most important thing—to believe in myself.

I am a Sort-bot. It is my job to sort—and to create.

THE END

I Have a Clone

Hard Work

"TRIXIE, COME DOWN AND DO THE DISHES," yelled one of Trixie's dads. Trixie sighed and started walking downstairs, but Trixie didn't want to do the dishes, not one bit.

Trixie hated doing chores. She never saw any point in them. Especially cleaning. Everything just ended up dirty again!

Her other dad passed by while she was washing the dishes. "Nice job. Please sweep the lab when you are done."

UGGHHH Trixie couldn't believe she was getting more work. She had JUST done the dishes. But complaining wouldn't change anything. So she grabbed the broom and went down, down, down into the basement.

Trixie's dads were scientists and inventors. It was

awesome! They always made Trixie the coolest stuff.

Like the freeze gun she got for her fifth birthday.

Or the smart closet that picked out her outfits.

Or the hologram of the night sky on her ceiling.

So they could definitely make a robot to do the dishes or sweep the lab or to make the bed. But no matter how much she asked, they never did. They always told her, "When you are older, you will understand."

Trixie hated that answer.

As she was sweeping, Trixie looked around the lab. There was a bunch of cool stuff in there. Like a flamethrower and a spaceship and a goo-ifier. All of them had signs that said, "DANGER. KEEP OFF. THIS MEANS YOU, TRIXIE."

But then Trixie saw a new machine in the lab.

It was big. It was gray. And there wasn't a danger sign on it.

Trixie was curious. Really curious. Really, really, really curious.

She put one foot in, then another, then another, then another. Nothing had exploded so far, so Trixie stepped in more and more. She got to the middle of the machine. Then, suddenly, it turned on!

ZAP

A green light hit her!

Trixie ran out of the machine as fast as she could. She was heading upstairs when she heard, "Hello."

It was her voice, but she wasn't speaking. Trixie turned around and came face to face with herself!

WHOA!!!

"I am your clone. It is nice to meet you," said the other Trixie.

"What does that mean?" the first Trixie asked.

"It means I am a copy of you," responded the Clone.

"So you are like my twin?"

"Similar," said the Clone, "but I have to follow your directions."

"AWESOME!" yelled the first Trixie.

Trixie made the clone do everything she didn't want to.

Trixie had the Clone sweep the lab.

Trixie had the Clone do the dishes.

Trixie even had the Clone go to school.

The Clone was doing everything Trixie was supposed to, but she was doing them better.

Her dads were so proud of everything 'she' was doing that they even got her a dog!

Trixie named him Max. She had the Clone take care of him too.

All Trixie had to do was to hang out and relax.

And that was just how Trixie liked it.

Everything was going just as Trixie wanted.

Until one day, when Trixie was home alone. The Clone was at school for her, and her dads were at work. Trixie wanted to go swinging. She ran outside as quickly as she could. She swung pretty high. She kept swinging higher, and higher, and higher, until she could touch the clouds.

But then, out of the corner of her eye, she saw the dog run out of the house!

Trixie had forgotten to close the door.

She jumped off the swing and ran after the dog.

But she couldn't catch him.

She called him, but he wouldn't come.

Trixie started to cry; she didn't know what else to do.

But then, Trixie saw something in the distance.

It was her clone, and walking next to her, was the dog!

When they came close enough to talk to, Trixie asked, "How come he came to you but not me if you are my clone?"

"I think it's because I was taking care of him," said the Clone, "It was hard work. But hard work has its benefits. Everything you made me do was hard work. But it had to get done. Hard work makes you grow."

From then on Trixie looked at her clone in a new light. She realized how much stuff the Clone could do that Trixie couldn't. The Clone could make sandwiches and breakfast, Trixie couldn't. The Clone could do long division, Trixie couldn't. Trixie didn't even know where the dog food was.

Trixie told the Clone, "I'm sorry I made you do all of those things. From now on you can do whatever you want."

The Clone responded, "But what about all of your chores?"

"I think it's time I started doing my own chores," Trixie said. "Maybe I need some hard work in my life."

THE END

Unusual Help from Smartphones

Honesty

Jack and Jimmy are the best of friends.

They do absolutely everything together.

They always sit next to each other in class.

They always know how the other feels, without having to ask.

And they always have all the same stuff.

So when Jimmy got a phone, well, Jack just had to have one too.

But these phones weren't like all the others. These phones were a new type of phone. They were specifically designed for kids. They already had built-in child protection.

Kids couldn't do just anything with these phones. In fact, the kids couldn't make the phone do anything at all.

Yet somehow, these phones knew when you were in trouble and always knew just who to call.

If you scraped your knee and needed your mom to help it feel better, the phone would call her.

Or if you were near a fire, it would just call 911.

The phone knows what the kids need and does it.

It is as simple as that.

Jack and Jimmy love their new phones, but what Jack and Jimmy love most is to explore.

Every day after school, Jack and Jimmy go into the little bit of woods in Jimmy's backyard.

They fence with sticks.

They climb on rocks.

They run under the trees, and they smile at the feeling of the wind rushing past their faces.

They have a whole world out there.

A world all their own. They are the kings of it.

They don't have any rules. They don't need any because Jack and Jimmy never, ever fight.

One day, Jack spotted something, "Jimmy, there is a lizard right there. It looks like it is hurt. Should we take it home?"

Jimmy was about to say yes, when both of their phones started talking.

"Calling mom."

"Huh," Jack said, "I guess our phones think we should ask our moms before bringing home a hurt lizard."

Jimmy nodded, "Weird."

They asked their parents, and they said yes!

They named the lizard Norbert and nursed it back to health. They shared Norbert, and traded-off with him every week.

It was awesome!

But then, one day Jack had a cold. He couldn't go to school, but Jimmy could.

Jimmy didn't want to go without Jack, but he had to go to school. His mom said so.

It just so happened that a new student arrived that day.

This new student sat down right next to Jimmy.

His name was Leo.

Jimmy and Leo talked all day.

They became such good friends that after school, Jimmy took Leo to the woods behind his house.

There they played.

And climbed up rocks.

And ran so fast, they felt like they would fly.

All the things that Jimmy and Jack would do.

Just without Jack.

When Jack felt better, Jimmy thought that he would be so excited to meet Leo.

But Jack wasn't.

Jack was angry. Whenever the three of them hung out, Jack was mean. So the three of them stopped hanging out. Jimmy and Leo would play in the woods after school, without Jack.

Jack said that this didn't bother him. Jack said that he didn't want to be friends with Jimmy anymore. Jack said that he was happy without him. Jack was lying.

A couple of weeks passed by; Jack and Jimmy only saw each other to trade-off Norbert. They didn't even talk to each other in class. Jack was sad. Really sad. He missed his very best friend.

"*Calling Jimmy*" said his phone. *Oh no,* Jack thought, he did not want to talk to Jimmy. Well, actually he did, he just didn't want Jimmy to know that. Just as Jack was about to cancel the call, Jimmy picked up.

"Jack," Jimmy said, "I'm so glad you called. I miss you."

Jack sat for a moment. Then he decided to be honest, "I miss you too, Jimmy. I'm sorry that I was so mean. I was jealous of Leo. I thought you liked him more than me."

"It's okay, Jack. I like Leo, but you are my best friend. That will never, ever change. Do you want to come over and play in the woods?"

And Jack went over to play in the woods.

They jumped on rocks.

And fenced with sticks.

And ran so fast nothing could catch them.

It was just like before, but better.

Because sometimes Leo would come over too, and Leo was pretty cool.

Jack actually really liked Leo, and they all became good friends.

And whenever fights came up, because they always do, they were honest about what was really bothering them. Because if you want things to get better, the first step is being honest. People can't help you if you don't tell them what is wrong. And you can't fix anything without knowing what the problem is.

THE END

Search for a New Home for the Inhabitants of Planet Ko

Sense of Responsibility

There is a planet named Ko,
It isn't all that far from wherever you are.
And I promise that wherever you go,
You can see Ko in the night sky; it looks like a star.

Ko is a very nice planet.
It's a purple-y, green-y color.
Everything had ears like a rabbit.
And it was always hot like summer.

The people of Ko had been there a long time,
So long, in fact, that they had a problem.
The number of people on the planet started to climb.
This isn't a problem by its lonesome.

But since the planet didn't grow, too,
They were starting to run out of space.
This was a bit of an issue,
So they had to look for a new place.

But they had an idea to help,
A way to save them.
It would be their next step
To make a ship to send to a new realm.

They got to work building the ship,
They were afraid it would be the last thing they did
So they loaded it with a bunch of stuff for the trip
They told it about all the things they had built.

They taught it about music,
Everyone on Ko loves a flute.
They told it which flowers to pick.
And how to grow the best fruit.

They made something truly amazing,
But there was one catch.

It could feel, it was living,
And he didn't want to leave; he loved Ko too much.

Whenever he thought about going,
His engine would freeze up.
He loved Ko so much, he thought about staying.
But he knew he had to go; he was stuck in a slump!

He was just so scared to go,
And didn't want to be alone.
It made him feel so low.
Here was all he had ever known.

This is very understandable,
It is hard to do something new
Even if you know in every single cable,
That it's something you have to do.
And the stars looked so far away,
So cold, and so lonely,
So here he wanted to stay.
He felt like such a phony!

He was supposed to fix stuff.

But it wasn't his fault the planet was small.

It wasn't his fault life is rough.

Why should it be his problem at all?

Why did they make him?

It was their problem, not his.

But he looked at everyone around him,

They would suffer if he didn't fix this.

He was flying around town,

Trying to find a way to get this done.

He searched everywhere, looking up and down.

When he saw a girl helping someone.

She gave her lunch to someone else,

To someone who needed it more.

He asked her why, and she told him this,

"I could help, so I did; it wasn't a chore."

He thought this was very interesting.

He thought about it all day and night.

The more he thought the more he was believing,
Maybe this kid was right!

When things go wrong,
Or a problem needs to be solved,
Someone has to step up and be strong,
Someone has to get involved.

You can't just ignore a problem,
The longer you take to get to it,
The worse you tend to find them.
You have to face it with grit.

You still have to clean up the mess you make,
But if you can, maybe help your partner too,
Because maybe one day you will make a big mistake,
And you will need someone else to help you.

The people of Ko
Needed help to save them.
And the ship was finally ready to go,
And find them a new home.

It was lonely work,
And sometimes he got sad.
But it had a perk,
He knew he was making people glad.

The ship had already learned about music and art
It had learned about history and math
But taking responsibility—that was hard,
And to get something done, someone has to walk
the path.

Someone had to take charge,
Someone had to put themselves last.
So he went into a world so large,
Trying to find a new home for them fast.

He flew past a million planets that just wouldn't do.
Some were even smaller.
There were some where nothing grew.
But he was a good explorer.

There had to be something just right,
Then finally he found it.

He couldn't believe his sight!
There, at the end of the world, was the perfect fit!

It was a green-y, yellow-y planet,
Where fruit grew as big as canyons.
He knew they would love it,
Since the flowers grew as tall as mountains.

He went back to get the people of Ko.
It was time for them to get a new place to call their own.
What they would name it, he didn't know,
But he hoped that everyone would just call it home.

THE END

Printed in Great Britain
by Amazon

79484399R00039